FOREST
OF
FAITH

Bedtime
with
JESUS

Finding REST in HIS LO

by Susan Jones

Illustrated by Estelle Corke

Good  Books

New York, New York

The *forest* is quiet as the sun rises.
But Little Bunny can't sleep one wink more.
She peeks out to see whether Mama is up
and about yet.

Suddenly, the quiet is broken as
Little Bunny bounds into the garden.
"Mama, it's almost the big day!"

"Have you come up with
an answer to my very
important question?"
Mama asks.

Little Bunny grins widely as she blurts out, "A sleepover under the stars—with *food* and games and *friends!*"

Mama smiles back. "What a great way to celebrate your birthday! Let's start planning."

Little Bunny makes invitations and hops along to deliver them to her friends.

The days until the sleepover seem to take *forever!* But *finally,* tonight *is* the celebration.

Mama decorates a special birthday carrot cake.

Papa paints a spectacular birthday banner.

Everyone is ready for a super night!

As the sun sets, Little Bunny's friends arrive with excitement and their sleeping bags.

What should the friends do first?

They play fun games of tag and kickball.
They eat slices of birthday cake. Yum!

They even have a silly dance contest.
And now it's time to settle in for the night.

Everything is still ... until a gust of wind rustles some leaves. The friends cry out: "What was that noise?" "I can't sleep!" "Me either!"

"I know just what will help—good night wishes!" says Mama, as she offers comforting pats and big, warm hugs.

Everything is quiet again ... until
a branch snaps somewhere nearby.

The friends jump up, but Papa comes
running to the rescue with a book.
"Let's try a bedtime story to fill our
heads with happy thoughts!"

As Papa reads peacefully, everyone starts to feel calm. Until an owl hoots in the distance!

What now? They planned everything to make this a special celebration! But no one will be happy if they can't get some sleep. Mama looks up at the night sky and lets out a big sigh. Then, suddenly, an answer comes.

"I know why we're having trouble getting some rest," says Mama. "We forgot one very special invitation to this sleepover: to Jesus!"

"Can we talk to him now, Mama?" Little Bunny asks. "Yes, let's pray!" Papa agrees. "All we need to do is say how we're *feeling* or what we need."

One by one, the animals talk to Jesus. "Jesus, help me know that those sounds are just the nighttime in the forest," prays Little Skunk.

"Jesus, help me *feel* your good night hug as I pull my sleeping bag tight around me," prays Little Hedgehog.

"Jesus, help settle that second piece of cake in my belly!" prays Little Raccoon.

"Mama, I don't know what to say to Jesus,"
says Little Bunny.

"It can be as simple as, 'Jesus, be with me,'"
Mama says. "Or we can try a bedtime prayer
I learned when I was a little bunny."

Now I lay me
down to sleep,
I pray the Lord
my soul to keep.
May angels watch me
through the night
And wake me with
the morning light. Amen.

"No matter what words we use to talk to Jesus, he knows our hearts and just how to calm our fears. We can rest in his love," says Papa.

"That's a very special gift!" says Little Bunny as she yawns and smiles at the sleepy circle of friends.

Good Books
307 West 36th Street, 11th Floor
New York, NY 10018

Good Books books may be purchased in bulk at special discounts for sales promotion,
corporate gifts, fund-raising, or educational purposes. Special editions can also be
created to specifications. For details, contact the Special Sales Department,
Good Books, 307 West 36th Street, 11th Floor, New York, NY 10018
or info@skyhorsepublishing.com.

Good Books is an imprint of Skyhorse Publishing, Inc.®, a Delaware corporation.

Visit our website at www.goodbooks.com.

10 9 8 7 6 5 4 3 2

Library of Congress Cataloging-in-Publication Data is available on file.

Illustrations by Estelle Corke

Print ISBN: 978-1-68099-836-8
Ebook ISBN: 978-1-68099-849-8

Printed in China